Miss Biddlewick gets even WITH SANTA!

Donna & Eve Shavatt

American Literary Press, Inc.
Shooting Star Editions
Baltimore, Maryland

Miss Biddlewick gets even With Santa

This book is dedicated to John and Drew for their unwavering encouragement and support; and, of course to Mom and the rest of our family.

Library of Congress
Cataloging in Publication Data
ISBN 1-56167-480-X

Library of Congress Card Catalog Number:
98-88360

Published by

Shooting Star Editions
American Literary Press, Inc.

Miss Biddlewick was a cleaner of houses
whose face wore the *vilest* frown
Who would think such a bitter old woman
could live in *a place called TWINKLETOWN?*

But even though she was quite mean and hateful
and even though her expression was ghastly
There was a reason for Miss Biddlewick's demeanor
you see, she wasn't *always* so nasty

When she was just a little girl
a letter to Santa she wrote
Then she waited with anticipation
for him to acknowledge her note:

MY CHRISTMAS WISH LIST

Dearest Santa, I have only one wish

That would fill me with joy from bottom to top

I want it more than anything else in the world

Please Santa, can I have the doll called Babyteardrop?

XOXOXO,

Bobbi Biddlewick

But something went terribly awry
that fateful Christmas day
She got a gift she would NEVER have asked for
and she vowed that Santa would pay!

As she cleaned from one house to another
she'd see children making their lists
Then they'd send them off to Santa Claus
their faces filled with bliss

Every year it just made her madder
when they got what they desired
But she kept those feelings to herself
'cause that could get her fired!

For forty years she plotted
for forty years she schemed
At last her plan came together
even *better* than she dreamed

She waited 'til Christmas Eve
to get even with Mr. Claus
What she had in mind for the children
would give old Santa pause!

The first step was to make a batch
of sticky green Goobledeegop
She'd pour it in the children's stockings
from the toe up to the top!

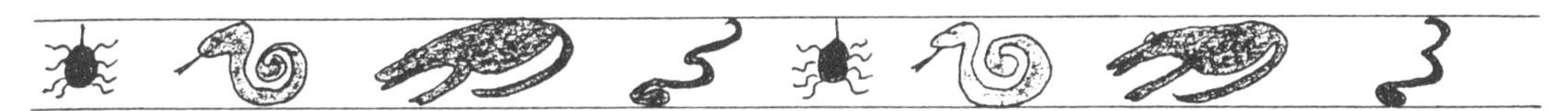

She made a beeline for the kitchen
pulled out all her pots and pans
Miss Biddlewick didn't even bother
to wash her dirty hands!

To get the right mix of nastiness
in when a little of this and of that
She stirred it all together
then added lint from in her hat

A pinch of yuck, a dash of gook
for just the right shade of green
As the *Grand Finale*, some gum from her shoe
What a wonderfully horrid cuisine!

She then took a large plastic bag
and filled it with the slimy green slop
she put it aside until she was ready
to deliver her Goobledeegop

To dine on cookies and milk
she knew Santa loved to do
So she'd eat them all herself tonight
and *HE'D* go hungry... *Well, boo hoo hoo!!!*

She dressed up to look like Saint Nick
hooked her housecleaning keys to her hip
Slung the Goobledeegop over her shoulder
then took off at a mighty fast clip

While Santa's sleigh approached a rooftop
into that home she did slink
and headed straight for the cookies and milk
which she proceeded to eat and to drink

Next she tucked herself into a closet
as Santa placed presents 'round the tree
Then as he made his way back up the chimney
she swapped name tags on every gift she could see!

Then quick as a flash she poured Goobledeegop
into a stocking that hung there with care
Then she moved on to the one next to that
and repeated the process in there!

To top it all off she tiptoed upstairs
to where everyone was sleeping like rocks
Then she delayed the time for awakening
on all of the kid's alarm clocks!

And on to the next house just before Santa
first, to eat and to drink what was his
Then once more, to hide and to wait
to mix up nametags of parents and kids!

More Goobledeegop, more messed-up clocks
then on to the next house she went
Finally every house in town was mixed up and glopped
and all of her anger was spent!

She'd made sure *NO ONE* in all of Twinkletown
would get what they had asked for
She had gotten revenge on old Santa
she had *FINALLY* evened the score!

Meanwhile, at the North Pole
Mrs. Claus was doing some baking
When her oven, old and worn out
started knocking and smoking and shaking!

The North Pole's oven replacement crew
pulled the broken down stove out with care
and were putting the new one in place when they heard
"No, wait! There's an envelope down there!"

Mrs. Claus reached for the letter she had spotted
and to help her see she lit a candlestick
"Oh my!" she fretted as she opened it up
"It's a wish list from a child named Bobbi Biddlewick!"

It read "My Dearest Santa, I have only one wish
that would fill me with joy from bottom to top
I want it more than anything else in the world
Please Santa, can I have the doll called BabyTearDrop?"

Well, it was clear that this poor little child
did not get what her letter asked for
Because according to the faded old postmark
it had spent forty years there on the floor!

Mrs. Claus did some pretty fast thinking
an emergency e-mail she sent
When Santa heard the urgent beeping
off to his sleigh for his computer he went

Her e-mail explained what she'd found
so Santa scanned back to that day
When he entered the name of Biddlewick
"NO WISH LIST RECEIVED!" It did say!

Now Santa felt badly indeed
so he backtracked to the town called Twinkle
This time Bobbi Biddlewick would get what she'd asked for
and his plan worked with nary a wrinkle

As he placed a brand new BabyTearDrop
under Miss Biddlewick's lonely tree
He added a note to explain and apologize
thinking, "I surely hope she forgives me!"

As a result of Miss Biddlewick's shenanigans
here's what happened on Christmas day
Everyone got someone else's gift...
it was truly mixed up I must say:

Bob's mixed-up gift was a small pink box
with a ballerina dancing on top
But that was no more sillier
than Mrs. Turner's Robo Cop!

Giving Mable her daddy's new suit
was preposterous indeed
But no crazier than a dictionary
to baby Beth who couldn't read!

Billy was simply shocked
when he unwrapped Mary's new dress with lace
While Heather, at age 4,
opened a genuine leather briefcase!

Mr. Adams had just opened
Isabella's CandyLand
While Mrs. Adams looked confused
at her new *Barbie-On-A-Stand*!

And what was *Henry* gonna do
with *Cindys jewelry box*
And what could Sally do
with Mr. Johnson's new *tube sox*?

Mrs. Carter tore the wrapper
off a bike with training wheels
While Jeffrey scratched his head
at his strange gift of blue high heels!

Little Angie was NOT happy
with brother Markie's Ninja Turtle
And you shoulda seen Sammy's face
when he unwrapped grandma's girdle!

Christmas morning Miss Biddlewick awoke
to the noisiest, jolliest racket
Before she went out to investigate
she slipped into her boots and her jacket

Suddenly she spotted the shiny bright present
underneath of her Christmas tree
She was stunned! And thought to herself
"Why, this just can't be a present for *me*!"

When she finally tore open the wrapper
read the note, and gazed at the doll
She felt all her bitterness just float up and away
this was simply the *best* Christmas of all!

And you really won't believe what had happened
it was simply the strangest thing
The children were playing with the Goobledeegop
which made fun noises, like Plop Plop! and Pong Ping!

Plus, the Goobledeegop could be molded
into trucks, into dolls, into boats!
What's more, it glowed in the dark
and it could bounce, it could fly, it could float!

So the mixed up gifts were corrected
and the Goobledeegop was a hit
The kids were even up early
they didn't need alarm clocks one bit!

Miss Biddlewick went back to her rocker
and she cuddled her BabyTearDrop
She felt bad about eating the cookies,
so she jumped up from her chair with a pop!

To the kitchen she ran to begin
baking cooKies like never before
Snickerdoodles, Thumbprints, Oatmeal Raisin
she baked dozens and dozens and more!

She packaged them up in a huge box
and inside she'd written a line
That read, "Santa, these are for you dear,
and the pleasure, it truly was mine!"

Then she looked out her window and noticed
her new neighbor was just moving in
She had with her a five-year old daughter
just adopted that morning at ten!

Miss Biddlewick scooped up her doll
combed it's hair, and tied on a bow,
With a smile she gave it to the little girl
who said, "Oh thank you, I do love her so!"

When she was happy Miss Biddlewick was quite lovely
and her life was forever made better
She had learned the *TRUE* meaning of Christmas
Which had *NOTHING* to do with that letter!